The Mummy Shop Catalogue

Hundreds of mummies to choose from! ORDER NOW, CALL TODAY!

For K & E, and for my mummy
A.L.

To my mum and Aunt Eileen
L.B.

This edition published in 2019
First published in 2013 by Scholastic Children's Books
Euston House, 24 Eversholt Street
London NW1 1DB
a division of Scholastic Ltd
www.scholastic.co.uk
London – New York – Toronto – Sydney – Auckland
Mexico City – New Delhi – Hong Kong

Text copyright © 2013 Abie Longstaff
Illustrations copyright © 2013 Lauren Beard
PB ISBN 978 1407 192 30 7

SCHOLASTIC

THE MUMMY SHOP

Written by
Abie Longstaff

Illustrated by
Lauren Beard

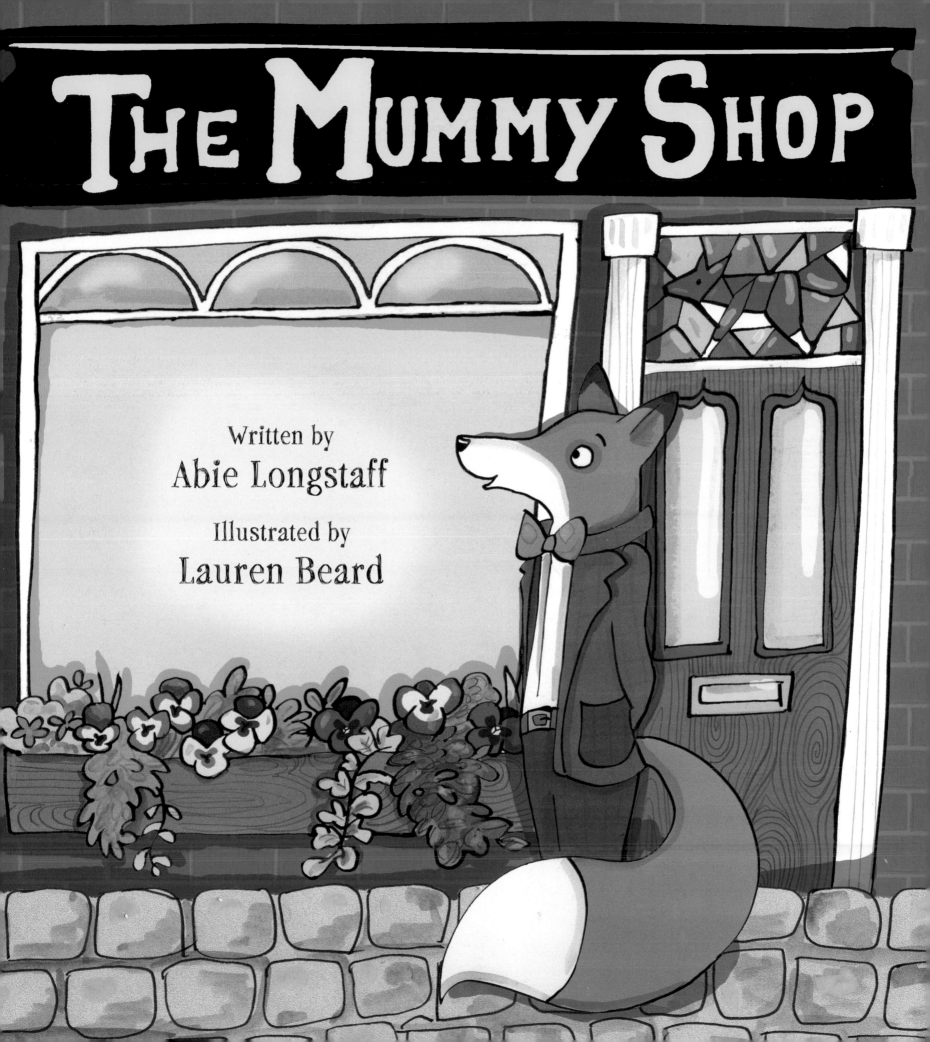

One day my mummy made me **very** cross.

I had to tidy my room **all** morning,

she made me help in the supermarket **all** afternoon,

and at night-time, I had only just started playing when she made me brush my teeth and go to **bed!**

I was cross,
cross,
cross!

But the next day I saw something in the newspaper.

I took a deep breath and dialled the number.

Ring ring!

A friendly voice answered.
"Good afternoon, The Mummy Shop, how may I help you?"

"Hello, I'd like a new mummy please,"
I said with my best manners.
"Of course, sir!" said an excited voice,
"I'll have a new mummy for you in no time!
Now, may I ask what is wrong with your own mummy?"

"No bouncing? That is very grave indeed, sir," said the shop owner. "I'll just look through my books… Aha! I have the **perfect** mummy for you! She will bounce with you all day long!"

"Hooray, I'll take her! Thank you," I said.
I couldn't wait for my perfect mummy to arrive.

My new mummy was fun, but she wasn't **quite** perfect.

Ring ring!

"Good afternoon, The Mummy Shop, how may I help you?" said the owner, brightly.

"Hello, I'd like to return this mummy please," I said. The owner seemed surprised. "Oh **really**, sir? Was there a problem?" he asked.

"Well," I said, "she **did** let me play all day and she's definitely very bouncy, but…

…it turns out she can only cook carrots. We had…

and carrot
ice cream!

carrot
jelly

carrot
cake

carrot
pie

It was **horrible! My** mummy cooks really, really well," I explained.

"Oh dear, sir… But don't worry. I have the **perfect** mummy for you! She is a sheer delight and also an excellent cook. I'll send her round right away!" the owner announced.

More Mums

MUMMIES VOL. 2

MUMMIES FOR YOU

MUMMIES VOL. 3

MUMS, MUMS & MUMS

My new mummy was great at juggling **and** cooking...
but she wasn't perfect either.

So I phoned the shop again. The same voice answered.

"Good afternoon, The Mummy Shop, how may I help you?"

"Hello," I said quietly, "I'm afraid this mummy didn't work out for me after all."

The shop owner gasped. "But what was the matter **this** time, sir?"

"Well," I said, "she **did** play with me all day and she **did** cook a lovely lunch, just like I wanted. But…

…she makes me wear scratchy clothes all the time. I've worn woolly jumpers, woolly trousers and even **woolly underpants!** They all tickled and itched, not like the clothes **my** mummy buys."

"How very uncomfortable!" the owner said. "But never fear!
I will find the **perfect** mummy for you, sir!… Oh yes, here's one!
She even makes clothes — oh, she's incredible with her needles!"

"OK," I shrugged, "I guess I'll try her. Thank you."

This mummy was lots of fun and she didn't mind mess, but there was yet **another** problem.

"Good afternoon, The Mummy Shop, how may I help you?"
said the familiar voice.

"It's me again," I sighed. "Thank you for the mummy you sent.
She **did** do everything you said she would: she played, she cooked,
she made me nice clothes, but…

...she doesn't like cuddling," I said sadly.

OUCH!

"Her needles prickled me all over! My mummy is soft and squidgy."

"Oh dear. Well, chin up, sir," said the owner. "Your **perfect** mummy is out there… now, let me see…"

There was a furious tapping at the keyboard, and suddenly he cried out,

"Yes! Perfect! She absolutely loves cuddling! No matter what she is doing, she will always have enough arms to cuddle you!" he said in triumph. "She's on her way now!"

I opened the door in excitement. WOW!

This mummy could play, cook **and** cuddle…

…but she still wasn't perfect.

And suddenly I knew what was wrong. I picked up the telephone one last time.

"Hello," I said, "I know this mummy does everything I asked for… but there's one problem."

"What is it, sir?" asked the owner.

"She's not **my** mummy. **My** mummy is the one who looks after me best of all. She knows my **favourite** dinner,

and plays my **favourite** games.

And at night-time, she tucks me in and reads me my **favourite** books."

"Well, sir," the owner smiled, "she sounds like your perfect mummy."
"She **is** my perfect mummy," I said, because finally I knew it was true.

And just then, the door opened...

And there was my mummy — my very own completely...

perfect mummy!